MAMA'S BOYZ

A second collection of
Mama's Boyz comic strips
by **Jerry Craft**

HOME SCHOOLIN'

Because learning shouldn't stop at 3 O'clock!

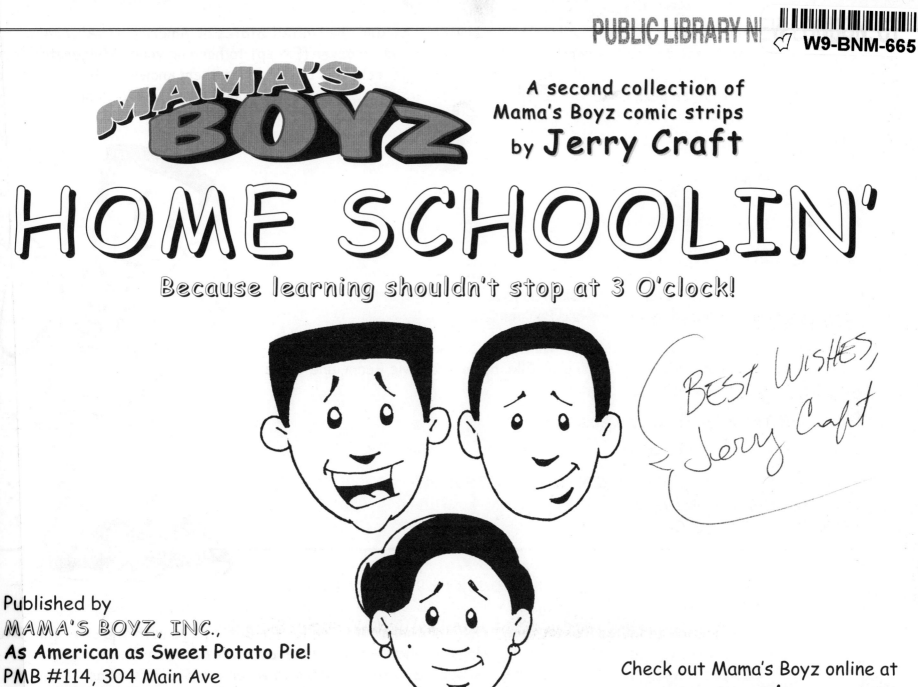

Best Wishes,
Jerry Craft

Published by
MAMA'S BOYZ, INC.,
As American as Sweet Potato Pie!
PMB #114, 304 Main Ave
Norwalk, CT 06851

Check out Mama's Boyz online at
www.mamasboyz.com

Mama's Boyz ©2007 by Jerry Craft. All rights reserved. Printed in the United States of America. USA! USA!
No part of this book may be used or reproduced in any manner whatsoever (Except to hang on your refrigerator door and stuff like that, but if you do it, make sure you tell folks it's from this book and let them know how to order their own copy) without written permission except in the context of reviews (Preferably good reviews). For more information, write to
Jerry Craft
Mama's Boyz, Inc.
PMB#114, 304 Main Ave,
Norwalk, CT 06851
or e-mail me at jerrycraft@aol.com

Printed in the USA

Layout, design, cover and everything else produced by Jerry Craft.
Jerry Craft was produced by Charles and Pauline Craft.

Editorial assistance by Autier Craft, Adrienne Hayward and Lissy Newman. Plus
big props to my junior editorial staff: Peter Elkind, Dani & Davie Beam, and Jaylen &
Aren Craft. You guys all did a great job!

Check out the Mama's Boyz website at:
www.mamasboyz.com

Library of Congress Catalog Card Number: 2007903247
ISBN-13: 978-0-9796132-0-3
ISBN-10: 0-9796132-0-5

Other books by Jerry Craft:

Not sure if I'm supposed to list books that I've DONE, or those that I've READ. But let's go with the ones that I've
DONE. Which so far is just one. **Mama's Boyz: As American as Sweet Potato Pie!**
But you can also see Mama's Boyz in *Chicken Soup for the African American Soul* as well as
Chicken Soup for the African American Woman's Soul and
The Complete Idiot's Guide to Comedy Writing

Me and the Boyz

Jerry Craft

Hi, I'm **JERRY CRAFT**, creator of **Mama's Boyz.** Welcome to my second collection of Mama's Boyz comic strips. I got such a great response from the first book: *Mama's Boyz: As American as Sweet Potato Pie!* that I thought I'd do it all over again. For those of you who are interested, I thought I'd tell you a little about myself and my career. I grew up in a section of New York City called Washington Heights, which begins right where Harlem ends. I am the youngest of three kids, and not by a little either. My brother and sister are 9 and 10 years older than me, so at times it was like I was an only child.

There was nothing like the neighborhood where I grew up. It was great! We were like the *Little Rascals*, a group of 10-15 kids who got up early to ride our bikes, go to the local basketball court or play stickball. After that, we'd head off to play softball or tackle football in the grass in front of Jumel Mansion. I'm sure the groundskeepers weren't too thrilled, being that it is a landmark and all, but that was all the grass we had!

My folks were always big on me getting a good education, so they sent me to private school to have a different experience than my brother and sister had. I attended School on the Hill in Harlem and St. Matthew's Lutheran School in Inwood. Man, did I hate wearing those uniforms! Although I can't say that school was my favorite place, I always did well so I was usually on the honor roll. I never let the peer pressure to act stupid change me. We are the only folks who lie about our success BOTH ways. The ones who have *no* money talk about how they're *getting paid!* While the ones who come from nice neighborhoods and went to good schools want to pretend how *gangsta* they are. I'm proud of what I am and even prouder of what I am not! After graduating from the Fieldston High School in the Bronx, I went to the School Of Visual Arts in NYC. The way that I was raised, the thought of NOT going to college was NEVER an issue. I didn't have a choice even if I didn't want to go. I received my B.F.A. degree in advertising. After working as a copywriter for about ten years, I decided to look for jobs where I got to draw more. My next stop was working in the art department at King Features Syndicate. I've worked on comic books such as *New Kids On The Block* for Harvey Comics and Barbara Slate's *Sweet 16* for Marvel Comics. My comic strips and illustrations have appeared in *The Village Voice, Ebony Magazine, The New York Daily News, Essence Magazine* and the following books: *The Complete Idiot's Guide to Comedy Writing, Chicken Soup for the African American Soul* and *Chicken Soup For the African American Woman's Soul.* I've also illustrated book covers, board games and children's books. Awards include an *African American Literary Show Open Book Award* for best comic strip as well as awards from the American Diabetes Association and the DC Campaign to Prevent Teen Pregnancy. Nominations include a Glyph Award, and a new media award by the National Cartoonists Society.

Mama's Boyz is distributed by me, by the King Features Weekly Service (which goes to more than 1,500 newspapers around the world), and by Pages Editorial to name a few. In October of 2006, I left my job as Editorial Director of Sports Illustrated For Kids to start my own business, Mama's Boyz, Inc! Now I do what I love best, and get to spend a lot more time with my family. Check me out online for current updates, or find me on YouTube to check out some of my Flash animation. Thanks for your support!

www.mamasboyz.com | www.myspace.com/jerrycraft | www.comicspace/jerrycraft

Thank you, thank you, thank you!

To my parents for giving me the drive, education and work ethic which laid the foundation for my success and made me the person I am today. They provided me with a happy, stable childhood upon which to draw (get it? "draw"). In fact, "Mom" (Pauline Porter) is named after my Mom. And Gran'pa (Charles Tisdale) is named after my Dad (but with my Mom's maiden name).

...

To my wife, Autier, for picking up where Mom & Dad left off. Thanks to my sons Jaylen and Aren for providing me with plenty of material for my comics -- even if they don't realize it (so don't tell them, they'll wanna get paid!). Plus they all served as my editors.

...

To the rest of my family and my friends for their support and prayers: the Crafts, the Haqqs, the Fords, the Bascombs, and the Tisdales. A special *thank you* to everyone who bought a copy of the first *Mama's Boyz* book. I don't just mean the folks who *own* a copy, I mean the ones who BOUGHT a copy -- especially at the full $9.95 cover price (as opposed to the "hey, man, can you hook a brotha up?" price). Those are the folks who made it possible to do this book.

...

A king-sized thumbs up to Venetta Smith, Jim Clarke and David Cohea (King Features Syndicate) and Jae Berry Brown (Pages Editorial Services, Inc). A pat on the back to the following folks who helped me, or inspired me, to make the first *Mama's Boyz* book a success: Cartoonist Lynn Johnston (For Better or For Worse) who wrote my foreword, and Bill Crouch, Jr. and Ron Evry who wrote cover blurbs. Thanks to Eric Jerome Dickey, Angela Burt-Murray, and Pam Toussaint for writing blurbs for THIS book. Sam Stevens who did the original *Mama's Boyz* website. Vince George who did my Mama's Boyz sweatshirts. Also the *Chicken Soup for the African American Soul* crew: Lisa Nichols, Eve Hogan, D'ette Corona, Jack Canfield and Mark Victor Hansen; **The guys from ECBACC (East Coast Black Age of Comics Convention):** Yumy Odom, Maurice Waters, comic historian Prof. William Foster, Alex Simmons, David Walker, Howard Simpson, Rochon Perry, Roland & Taneshia Laird, Turtel Onli, Keith Knight, Dwayne McDuffie, John Jennings, Stanford Carpenter, Harvey Richards, Lance Tooks, and Dawud Anyabwile. **Superb salespeople:** Colette Brea, Jeannine Carter and Gerald Moore. **Beloved bookstore buddies:** James Fugate (Esowon Books), Marva Allen and Rita Ewing (Hue-Man Books), Nkiru Books, Indigo Books & Cafe, Bee Dozier Taylor, Janifer Wilson (Sisters Uptown Books), Carrie Coles (Dygnyti Books), Glenderlyn Johnson (Black Books Plus, Inc.), Pat, Donna & Traci (That Old Black Magic), Basic Black Books, Linda Pate (Precious Memories) and last but definitely not least, Trust from Nubian Heritage. **Super supporters:** Deborah Caviness, Sherelle Harris, Melanie & David Turner and the Henry family, Mary Ford, Adrienne and Walter Hayward, Rhonda Joy McLean, Arlene Lewis-Bascom, Mabel Ivory, Ginger Nocera & Brenda Rhodes Miller, Barbara Ellis, Y2K family, the Beam family, the Finleys, Diane Winston, Trisha Barron, Wendy Campbell (Campbell & Company), Gamaliel "Beenie" & Melanie Ballard and Ernie Villany. Margo and Trae Candelario, Doniashay Tyner, D.J. Rick, Laura Goertzel, Micah Jackson & "Sheils on Wheels." The folks at Essence magazine, MOCCA, Bob Kersey, Jane & Beverly (JBRH Advertising), Terrie Williams, Ossie Davis, Josie MacArthur, Diane Winston, Richard Minsky. **Creative cartoonists:** Bud Blake (Tiger), Ray Billingsley (Curtis), Jim Borgman (Zits), Barbara Slate (Sweet 16), Barbara Brandon (Where I'm Coming From), Brumsic Brandon (Luther), Jim Keefe (Flash Gordon), Morrie Turner (Wee Pals), Samuel Joyner, Tim Jackson, and Ted Shearer (Quincy). **Props to:** Daryl Cagle, Dan Poynter, Lynette Velasco, Dan Napolitano (Alfred University), Geralyne Lewandowski, Peter Kay, Kirsten Rasanen, Sandra Schmitt, Michele Yu, Carrie Smith, Yvette Hayward & Nancey Flowers, Eric Vetter, Mashea McGhee, Kesia Taylor, Natalie Alleyne, Greg Amos, Leighann Lord and Jim Mendrinos. Diane Eckert, Richard Wilson & Brad Elson. Paul Eberhart. Leah Kimmet, Alex Roehner and Chris Knight. Alonzo Virgil, Antonio Crawford, Ryan Greene, Lisa Whaley and yes, you too, Denise Washington. **Magnificent media mavens:** Cynthia Franklin and Lloyd Grant (Kip Business Report), David Astor, Rich Watson, Ken Gale, Kae Thompson, Imhotep Gary Byrd, Winston Majette, Beverly Copeland, Troy Johnson (AALBC.com), Terrance Dean, Ann Brown (the A-List) and Maurice Horn (100 Years of American Newspaper Comics). And to the many other newspapers and fans who support my work. And because I KNOW I'm gonna forget SOMEONE important, I'm adding this blank line below so I can write your name in when I see you. You ARE important, it's just that what had happened was.. uh.. I was on deadline, and my kids were sick and our pet mouse Fuzzy ran away (he's back now) and... well, you know. But thank you nonetheless, you ARE important! Maybe even MORE important because LOOK, you get YOUR name written by my own little hands:

To my very good friend and supporter (listed to the right):
I couldn't have done this without you. _____

MEET THE CHARACTERS

Hi, I'm **Pauline Porter**! (You can see my picture to the left.) I'm the mother of two teenage sons, and the owner of *Porter's Books*, our family bookstore. I opened it years ago with my husband Virgil (who has since passed away due to complications from diabetes). Below my picture is my oldest son, **Tyrell**. Handsome, isn't he? Tyrell is 18 years-old and a freshman in college. He's very kind and very smart, but a little on the shy side. Underneath him is my youngest son, **Yusuf**, who is 16 years old, and the exact opposite in some areas. Like his brother, he is kind, but he loves to be the center of attention. He's also very popular, extremely athletic, and a great dancer. But he's not the least bit modest.

Next to Yusuf is **Keisha**, a lovely young girl who works with me at the bookstore. Then there are my sons' friends. **Pee Wee**, **Ebony** and **Korey**. Let's just say that they *mean* well. But they're good kids... basically. On the bottom right is my baby brother **Greg**, or as the boys call him, "Uncle Greggo" -- a really good guy and a computer genius. The only thing he's not... is married. But hopefully the woman pictured above him will change things. That's his girlfriend **Avis**. She's the total package. Plus she's a psychologist!

And last but definitely not least, is **Gran'pa**, my dad Charles Tisdale, who is a retired chef and jazz lover! Dad and Greg are great role models for the boys. Which is something that all young people need.

So there you have it, please join us as we show you a year in our lives.
Thanks for visiting.

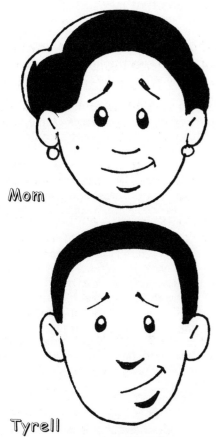

Mom

Tyrell

Yusuf

Keisha

Pee Wee

Ebony

Korey

Gran'pa

Avis

Greg

Back in the day

For any of you who are under 20 years old. I am about to tell you something that may just give you nightmares. When I was a kid, there was no such thing as the Internet!!! The first computer I ever saw was in my high school, it was HUGE but didn't do much of anything! So needless to say, NO ONE had them at home. That means no websites, no Google, no IM-ing. and no MySpace pages! Ordering online meant standing "on line" at the store. Email? Not a chance! Believe it or not, we even survived without cell phones, iPods... even call waiting. So if you tried to call me, and my sister was on the phone for six hours, there was NO WAY to reach me. All you'd get was a weird sound on the phone called a *busy signal*. Scary, huh? But I STILL had a lot of fun growing up.

Now let me take this time to say that the title **Home Schoolin'** does NOT mean that you shouldn't go to school! I am a HUGE believer in the power of a good education. No matter what you do. Even as a cartoonist, I can't tell you how much school has helped me in my career in both corporate America and as an artist. You may not realize it, but Mama's Boyz is as much about writing as it is drawing. Just look at what's on this page. If the best I could do was write stuff like: *"Me draw good, Momma's Boys am funny. By my buk."* you might think that this book just might be a waste of money. I need to be able to write my comics, write sales letters, ads... Plus, if I get interviewed by a newspaper or magazine, I have to know how to speak to them. They aren't going to quote me saying "know what I'm saying" after every sentence. Slang is cool when you're hanging out with friends, but unless you become a rapper, it probably won't do much in the business world. No one is going to hire you with a resume that says "yeah, I went to school sometimes, and now I wants a job, ya feel me?" And last but not least, don't forget math! I need to be able to figure out what my book and shirts will cost me to produce, what to charge, how to do my taxes, balance my budget. You name it. The more I know, the more I can do, and the less I have to rely on others.

In ADDITION to school, I also think that there is a lot of learning that needs to take place outside of school. That's what **Home Schoolin'** means. And I don't mean learning on the streets. Half the stuff you learn there is made to keep you there and never let you get ahead in life. A lot of what I learned as a kid came from home. My Mom showed me how important education was while my Dad gave me a strong work ethic. That means showing up on time and doing a good job. I learned not to let what other people thought of me keep me from being my own person. You can learn from ANYONE. Even from folks who DON'T do well. Man, most of the guys who I thought were so cool when I was a kid, turned out to be some pretty jacked-up adults. Years of smoking, drinking and drugs took a toll on them both physically and mentally. So not only did they end up with missing teeth, faded tattoos, and bruises that never really went away, but they never learned enough for them to do anything worth while once they got older. And the older they got, the worse off they became, because that type of life doesn't come with a 401K or a pension (money that's put away for you to use when you retire).

You can also learn a lot from your grandparents, uncles, teachers, coaches, ministers or neighbors just by talking to them. Our elders are the world's *best* history books. When my Dad was a boy, there were all kinds of things he couldn't do, and places that he couldn't go just because he was Black. And all kinds of awful names that folks called anyone who looked like him. The sad part is that now we call OURSELVES those same awful names!

What **Home Schoolin'** also DOESN'T mean, is staying home and schoolin' your friends on your Xbox or watching TV all day. Although we didn't have Xboxes and PlayStations back then, I did play with my Atari 2600. (And later, my Atari 5200. Man! That was a good system!) I also didn't have the option of watching cartoons 24 hours a day, seven days a week. This may give you more nightmares, but when I was a kid, the good cartoons came on ONE DAY each week. Saturday morning. Any others usually came on during the week after school. But those were always cartoons that hadn't had a new episode in over a decade. So if I missed Fat Albert on Saturday morning, that meant I had to wait seven LONG days to see the next episode! What we DID have though were friends. And comic books that made us use our imaginations. We couldn't BE Spider-Man in a video game or go to the movies to see him in action. But we had fun pretending to be him. We had plenty of other games to keep us busy, too. And something called "going outside to play." Yep, we used to come home from school, change into our *play clothes*, and actually LEAVE the house to play with other kids. Tag, freeze tag, jumping rope, hot peas 'n butter, stickball, or games like Skellies, also known as Skellzies or Lotees (Lo-tees), where we played with tops we'd make from two or three poker chips that were held together by melted bubble gum. Then we'd spend the day rubbing our top on the pavement in order to make it super smooth so it would go far. Now THAT was fun!

We could have fun with almost anything. Give us a ball and we played handball. Add a stick and it was stickball. And when there were no basketball hoops around, we used a garbage can or an old hat box and a volley ball. And I won't even get into all the games that came with opening a fire hydrant (I know some of you say fire plug). Boats made from twigs or matches raced down the stream of water heading towards Edgecomb Avenue. You learn by DOING, not sitting in your room all day. And you learn by listening to people. And you learn by trying new things. And hopefully, you learned a little something just now. I hope you enjoy hanging out with Mom and the boyz!

JANUARY

Gran'pa

I love this time of year. Not only the excitement of beginning a new year, but also to celebrate the birthday of Dr. Martin Luther King, Jr. It's because of men and women like him that today's African Americans can take advantage of their rights. Like voting! Even simple things like riding in the front of a bus, drinking from a water fountain that didn't say "colored only" or eating in restaurants without having to go through the *back* door or sit in the rear. It really wasn't that long ago that these things were just a dream. That's why whenever Dr. King's birthday rolls around, I always try to take Yusuf and Tyrell out to celebrate! And to show them that the lifestyle that they enjoy today came from a lot of hard work and sacrifice yesterday.

Flip the pages to watch Yusuf do his thing!

Note: Did you notice that I didn't use any lines to break up the four panels in this one? And there are no details in the background either. Gran'pa is actually floating in the air, but your mind makes you see a sidewalk. Cool, huh?

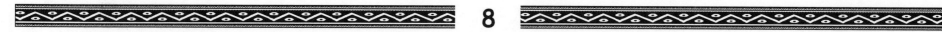

Note: This story inspired one of my readers to celebrate by going to a lunch counter just like Gran'pa and the boys.

the end

FEBRUARY

Mom

My favorite time of the year! That's because February is also known as **Black History Month**. Did you know that it began back in 1926 when Dr. Carter G. Woodson organized Negro History Week? It took place during the second week of February to celebrate the birthdays of Frederick Douglass and Abraham Lincoln. Now, it's a month-long celebration of our rich heritage. Our artists, writers, inventors, politicians, scientists... All the great people who have paved the way for us to succeed today. Plus it's a reminder that if they could do it, so can we! That's right, you, me, Tyrell... and yes, even Yusuf!

Note: There are no lines to divide the panels in any of the strips on these two pages either. Do you miss them?

MARCH

Keisha

Working with Mrs. Porter over the years has taught me a lot! Like celebrating **Women's History Month**. It's one of her favorite times, too. Along with February and, of course, September (when the boys go back to school). March was declared Women's History Month in 1987 in order to honor another group of people who helped to make this country great, but are also often overlooked. Women! Educators, artists, musicians, you name it... And speaking of musicians, last March, Mrs. Porter took the boys to see their first opera. I'm sure she knew it would never replace hip hop in their hearts, but like they say, you'll never know if you like something until you try it!

Emergency OPERA-tion

Note: I came up with this story while actually watching my first opera.

the end

APRIL

Yusuf

Well I like April for two reasons. The first is because it's spring. Which means that the weather is getting warmer and the days are staying lighter a whole lot longer. It won't be long til I can start playin' ball outdoors. Plus we get a spring break from school!

But the second is because I get to see Ma do her taxes. That's my revenge for all the times she tells me not to wait 'til the last minute to do things like my homework and term papers. So for me, it's really kinda fun to watch her running around crazy... I just make sure to do it from a safe distance. :)

Comment: Tax season is usually when Mom learns a few lessons of her own.

MAY

Tyrell

This is a cool month because Mother's Day reminds me and my brother to say "thanks" to Mom for taking such good care of us-- and not just when we were little, either. Even now, the stuff she has us do, like getting us to eat better, taking school more seriously, and working at the bookstore will probably make us better, smarter, healthier adults. Although we may not always agree with her decisions at the time. We got to pay Mom back a little last May when she got the flu right before Mother's Day. Taking care of her gave me and Yusuf a chance to really appreciate what she does for us everyday. Man, compared to what SHE has to do, we've got it easy!

SOUP-er Men

the end

Note: The two strips on this page, along with the one on the back cover, are three of my all-time favorites!

Comment: Yeah, they picked it up off the floor!

HOW I DRAW YUSUF

I do a *lot* of cartooning workshops for kids so I decided to put together a few tips for those of you who can't get to see me in person. Just keep in mind that this is how *I* like to draw. It's not a law, so you don't have to do it this way if it doesn't work for you. The important thing is to find what does work, then practice it. I STILL spend a lot of time practicing, and as a result, I feel like I'm still get better. When I was a kid, I began by tracing Spider-Man and the Silver Surfer out of my brother's comic books. Then when I got comfortable enough, I stopped tracing and tried to copy different pictures. Now I can draw almost anything I see just by picturing it in my mind first. But I also keep a file in my studio full of reference pictures that I cut out of magazines, just in case I need to see a specific picture. I have files of kids, cars, hip hop fashions and sports to name a few. Okay, enough talking, let's get stated.

1) I start with an oval, or an egg shape. It's hard to do perfect shapes, even for me, so I *sketch* out my pictures. That means that I connect a lot of little lines, then keep going over them til it's in the shape that I like. I start with light lines, then start to darken the ones that I like. It's almost like molding a lump of clay.

2) Next I add the shape of his hair on top. Then I draw a cross down the middle his head to help me place his features. The line that goes up and down (#1) is right in the middle. The one that goes side-to-side (#2), is a little higher than the middle. I add another line (#3) in between that and his chin. Take a look below to see what I mean.

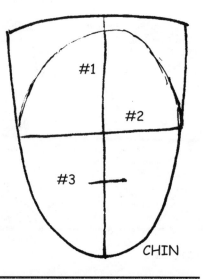

CHIN

3) Now I add his ears (just make the letter "C") so that line #2 is right in the middle of each ear. His eyes go on the same line. His nose goes on line #3. Now put a line in between his nose and his chin That will be his mouth. Take a look at the strip on page 89 to see how my style has changed over the years.

4) The last step is to go over the lines you like with a pen or marker. That's called inking. Then all that's left is to erase your guide lines. I use a blue pencil so I don't ever have to erase. I'll tell you more about that on the next page. Keep in mind that these are all EASY shapes. The head and eyes are eggs. The ears are the letter "C," and most of the other things are just simple curved lines.

NOTE: I do all of my drawing with a blue pencil. You can get the kind that looks just like a regular pencil (only they have blue lead). Or you can get a mechanical pencil and buy blue lead, which is what I do. The type of lead I use is a "non-repro" blue, which means that it does not reproduce. So once I have my drawing looking the way that I want, I go over the lines I like with a pen (or small brush) and India ink. Then when I go to make a photocopy or scan it into my computer, the blue lines don't show up, only the black ink lines. That way I never have to erase my pencil lines. So if I draw a car in the background then decide that I don't want it, I just don't ink over it. When I scan it, the blue car won't show up. I haven't erased in years! Which is great since I always used to rip my paper or get it really dirty. Don't you HATE when that happens? Oh, and I even have special paper that has my comic strip panel lines printed on them IN BLUE. That lets me know how big to make my strip and also gives me lines to help keep my lettering straight. You'll see samples on the next pages.

figure A

figure B

DRAWING THE FULL BODY: FIRST, DON'T LET ANYONE TELL YOU THAT DRAWING STICK FIGURES IS FOR BABIES! I start all of my people with stick figures. I just do an egg for the head, and eggs for the hands, feet, shoulders, knees and elbows (*see figure A*). It lets me see how the figure bends and makes sure that it always fits on my paper. That way I don't ever get to the bottom of the page and realize that I don't have enough room for his feet. Plus, if I want to change the way he's standing, I only have to redraw ONE line instead of a whole arm!

The other thing is that it gives my figures more motion. Look at the swooping lines for his body, arms and legs. This allows me to draw a cooler, more realistic, stance instead of a pose that's stiff and unnatural.

I normally come up with ideas for my strips just in the course of a regular day. I almost never sit down at my drawing table without a joke in mind.

Step 1: The first thing I do is write the words at the bottom, outside the panel. This helps me to figure out how much space I need for my lettering and where it will go. A lot of time I do the last panel first since this is where the big joke is. That's what's most important.

Step 2: I put in stick figures to see how the art will fit in with my word balloons and to make sure they fit in the panel.

Step 3: I start to put in my details like facial expressions and clothes, plus little things that will let you know right away that they are in a fast food joint. The cash register, trays, the menu, employees...

Personally I don't like my word balloons to cover any art, so I put them behind everything.
I'm also not going to put too much stuff behind the main action, because I don't want my joke to get lost. This is also a good time to try new things too, like the foot running out of the frame on the right.

Note: I have special paper that already has blue lines printed on it. It helps me to letter straight. And remember, when I scan it, none of the blue lines show up. The only reason you can see them now is because I made them really dark on purpose. How cool is that?!

Note: I always like how loose my sketches are. If I'm lucky my final version will keep a lot of the movement and the action that the first drafts have.

Step 4: When I have my comic layout the way I want it, I put it on my lightbox and place a sheet of my special paper or bristol board on top.

A lightbox is like those things that doctors use to look at x-rays. Once I turn it on, it lets me see the picture on the paper underneath in order to trace it with my fountain pen.

You can do the same thing by holding a drawing on a window and putting a new sheet on top. I use India ink for my comics because it doesn't fade away over time.

Step 5: Once I trace the drawing (only the lines I want), I begin to ink over my work, starting with the lettering. If you look above you'll see I also decided not to use certain things, like the running foot in the corner, and the items in the background. I just didn't think that they added to the joke. Now it's easier to focus on the action.

Final step: I scan it in my computer, then fill in the black areas like the hair and the pants. I also move some of the words over a bit and make some **bold** to stand out. The whole process takes me about two hours from start to finish.

JUNE

Uncle Greg

Well the boys love June because school is out for the summer. My sister, Pauline, hates June for the very same reason. I like it because of Father's Day. I think sometimes dads get overlooked, so it's always cool to make a fuss over my Dad and make sure he gets more than just ties, hankies and stinky cologne. Even though he never lets us do much more than that anyway. I'm lucky to have such a great dad, so I know how important they are. That's why we both try to spend a lot of time with Tyrell and Yusuf. Their dad passed away years ago (due to complications from diabetes), so we do whatever we can to try to help out. Especially since I understand what it's like to be a teenage boy. Now if I can just get them to put down the video games and go outside!

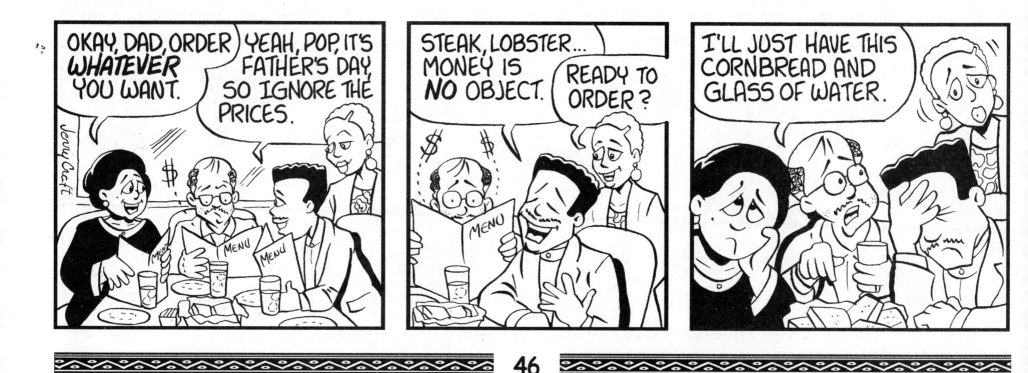

Comment: Back in the day, a "square" was someone who wasn't cool.

Back in the day: Before cable TV, we only had VHF or Very High Frequency (the regular channels) and UHF or Ultra High Frequency (channels like 47 and 88). Both were controlled by two different knobs on the TV. No remotes!

the end

JULY

Why do we LOVE July? Because it's the first full month of our summer vacation. NO school! We can sleep late, stay up late, play video games late... Plus the weather is nice so we can hang out and shoot hoops, or maybe even go to the pool. Then there's July 4th, where you can see fireworks and go to lots of cookouts. And the BEST movies usually come out now, too. You know, the summer blockbusters!!! July is the best month ever!!!

Pee Wee, Ebony and Korey

Comment: I always like when I can do an entire strip without using a single word!

August

Yusuf

I like August 'cause it's HOT! Man, summer is kickin' strong, so everyone is all about havin' a good time. As my uncle says, it's *Hot fun in the summertime! I think that's from some ol' song or movie or something. I love that I get to hang out with my friends. Plus Mom and Uncle Greg take off early from work or have summer Fridays, so I get to hang out with my family, too. It's cool 'cause we get to do stuff that we don't do other times of the year, like go to the beach, or have picnics and cookouts. The only bad thing is that each year you start seeing those "back to school" sales start earlier and earlier! Dag, that's just not right! But besides that, it's still a cool time of year.

Note: *Hot Fun in the Summertime is a classic song by Sly & the Family Stone.

Note: These are two one-panel strips. They are cool when I want to draw a lot of details in the scene. In both cases I used it to show how much stuff the boys have gotten into. See how many others are in the book.

Note: Some of my ideas for comic strips come from having conversations with people. This is one of them.

Note: Another idea that came from a conversation with a friend.

Note: I can use all sorts of things to get my point across. Look how the word "pow" along with action lines and a starburst show the force of their hands hitting. And in both strips I used a lightning bolt and stars to show pain.

SEPTEMBER

Why do we HATE September? Because it's the first full month of school. NO more summer vacation! We can't sleep late, can't stay up late, can't play video games all night. Plus the weather is startin' to get cool. And it gets dark fast so we can't hang out and play hoops. Even the pool is closed now. Labor Day weekend is the last bit of fun until the holidays start! Plus the movies that come out now stink!!! September is the WORST month ever!!!

Pee Wee, Ebony and Korey

Note: I ran the sentences together to show that Mom said the whole thing without stopping to take a single breath. It shows how excited she is to get them out of the house.

Note: This gag was sent in by a fan.

Note: I always like to show things that I enjoy in real life in my strips. BLACKJACK by Alex Simmons is one of my favorite comic books!

Note: Wavy lines around the border (like the last panel above), mean that someone is dreaming or imagining something.

the end

Note: This strip was reprinted in a magazine put out by the National Council of Teachers of Mathematics. Math rocks!!!

OCTOBER

Author Eric Jerome Dickey

I've made all kinds of appearances, but never in a comic strip. So when Mrs. Porter asked me to do a signing at Porter's Bookstore to celebrate **National Book Month,** I jumped at the chance (page 79). Hey, how can I refuse *Mom?* It was great to hang out with her and meet the boys. But now I know that I have to keep an eye on Yusuf in the future! I was glad to give Tyrell, and any young writer, the same advice that has helped me... Follow your dreams. Thanks, Mom!

-- *Eric Jerome Dickey*
New York Times and Essence Magazine bestselling author

THE 4-MONTH FEAST
by Pauline Porter

OCTOBER 31 is when it's **born,** hors d'oeuvres made of **candy corn**...

NOVEMBER'S appetizers then **drop by** with Thanksgiving dinner and sweet **potato pie!**

DECEMBER'S main course is not last, **nor least:** Christmas cookies and a **Kwanzaa feast!**

But in JANUARY I get my **just desserts** for eating and eating until it **hurts!** So I end my feast on the **grounds** of yet another resolution to lose *20 POUNDS!*

JERRYCRAFT@AOL.COM

Comment: Support you local bookstore! They are really important to the community!

Comment: I did this strip to show my support for my friend Lisa Nichols and the rest of my Chicken Soup family!

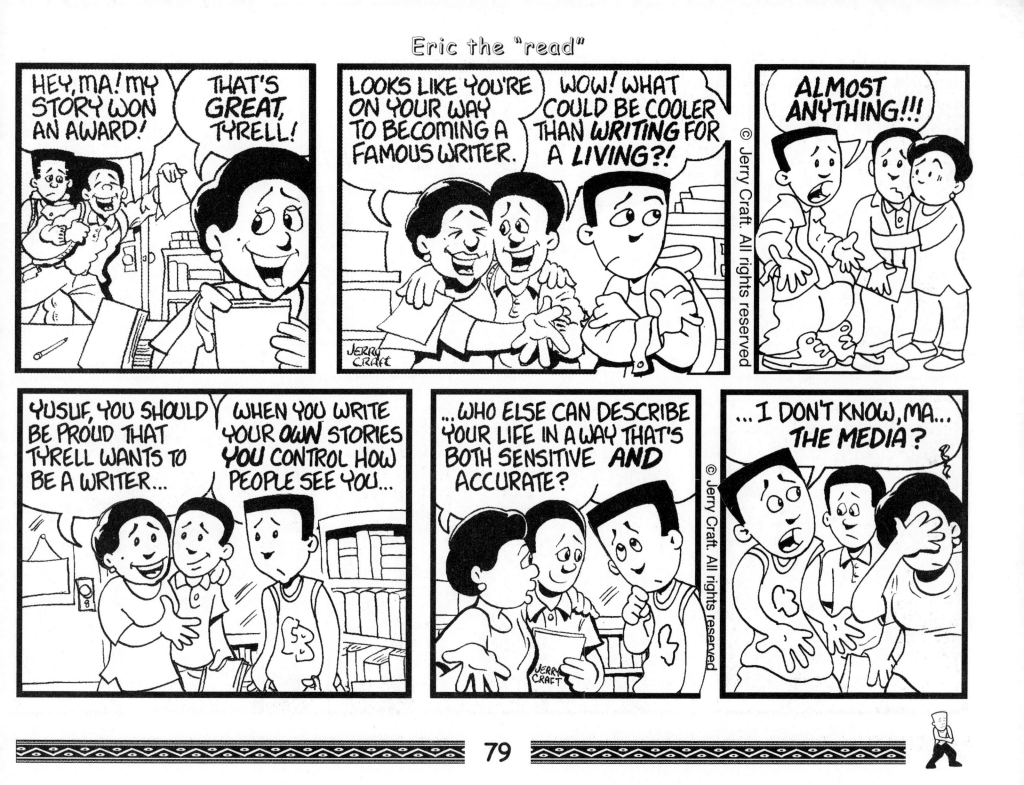

Note: Did you know that Eric has also written comic books? He did a six-issue Storm mini-series which was made into a graphic novel!

NOVEMBER

Avis

For me, this month is about taking time to be thankful and to count your blessings. One thing that I'm thankful for is how the Porters have invited me to share so many special times as a part of their family. Especially around Thanksgiving, since *Mom* can *really* burn in the kitchen!

She recently tried to teach Yusuf and his friends to have more respect for each other. You know, *more* compliments and *less* name-calling. As a psychologist, I know how important that it. If all you ever hear are insults and negative comments, eventually you may start to believe that they're true! I'm not so sure her lesson on self esteem went as well as planned though. But you be the judge.

My selfish team

YO, YUSUF, YOUR MOM'S HEAD IS *SO BIG* IT SHOWS UP ON RADAR!

YEAH! IT'S *SO BIG* SHE'S GOTTA STEP *INTO* HER TURTLENECKS!

OH YEAH?...WELL *MY MOM...*

IS RIGHT BEHIND YOU!

the end

Note: My style has changed a lot over the years. Check out how I used to draw their eyes and noses is the strip above.

DECEMBER

Mom

I love the holidays! The problem is that people put much too much pressure on themselves to buy gifts. Many African Americans spend too large a chunk of their yearly income on Christmas presents. It's crazy! No one should spend so much on presents that they have to struggle the rest of the year. Even though everyone LOVES presents, the pressure that comes along with having to pay a credit card bill, that you really can't afford to pay, can cancel out the good memories. For me it's better to live good for 12 months, then to live really good for ONE month, then have to struggle for the other 11. That's why we also celebrate Kwanzaa which is a great time to celebrate African-American culture. It's a wonderful time where the gifts are **not** the focus. They are educational or handmade, so we can enjoy it without adding to our family's credit card bill!

Pop quiz: Who would you rather be? Toasty-warm Tyrell? Or Yusuf and his crew who are all stylin'... but freezing?

'Twas the week before Christmas
and all through the store
Pauline Porter was working
to give her customers more.
So she arranged her books nicely,
both hard cover and soft
Then marked down the prices
to 20% off!
"Give books as gifts" she says,
"For pleasure and learning"
Instead of silly ol' gifts
that they'll end up returning!

For books are the gifts that keep on giving.
They bring knowledge and power,
and improve your living.
So she opened the door to let in the crowd
who was waiting outside,
and getting quite loud.
But the crowd was for NEXT door,
Mrs. Porter soon learned.
Something that made her very concerned.
Because it wasn't books
that the community wanted to see,
It was toys, DVDs and a PlayStation 3!

Note: Kwanzaa is a seven-day celebration that runs from the day after Christmas until New Year's Day.

Comment: See? This is what Mom was talking about before!

Me

I like to create comics and stories that do more than make you laugh. That's why I show Mom as a business owner, and as someone who is concerned with both health and literacy. I've created strips that tackle serious issues for clients such as the DC Campaign to Prevent Teen Pregnancy, the American Diabetes Association, Donate Life America, the NY Daily News' special AIDS supplement (below), Chicken Soup for the African American Soul, Chicken Soup for the African American Woman's Soul and others. You're also about to see a story which is both the most famous and infamous series that I've ever done. When it first ran in newspapers a few years back, a reader in Prince George's County got so upset that she demanded that her local paper stop running the story. And they did! It was the first time that ever happened, so I put the strips on my website to see what others thought. I received over 500 emails from parents, grandparents, teachers and church leaders thanking me for my work as well as a great write up in the Chicago Defender (Thanks, Tim)! So for this book I redrew the entire story to read more like a comic book instead of a series of strips. You can see more special strips on my website (www.mamasboyz.com)

American Diabetes Association

the end

FOR MORE INFO ON "AMERICA'S WALK FOR DIABETES" THIS OCT. CALL 1-800-254-WALK

Take a loved one to the doctor day

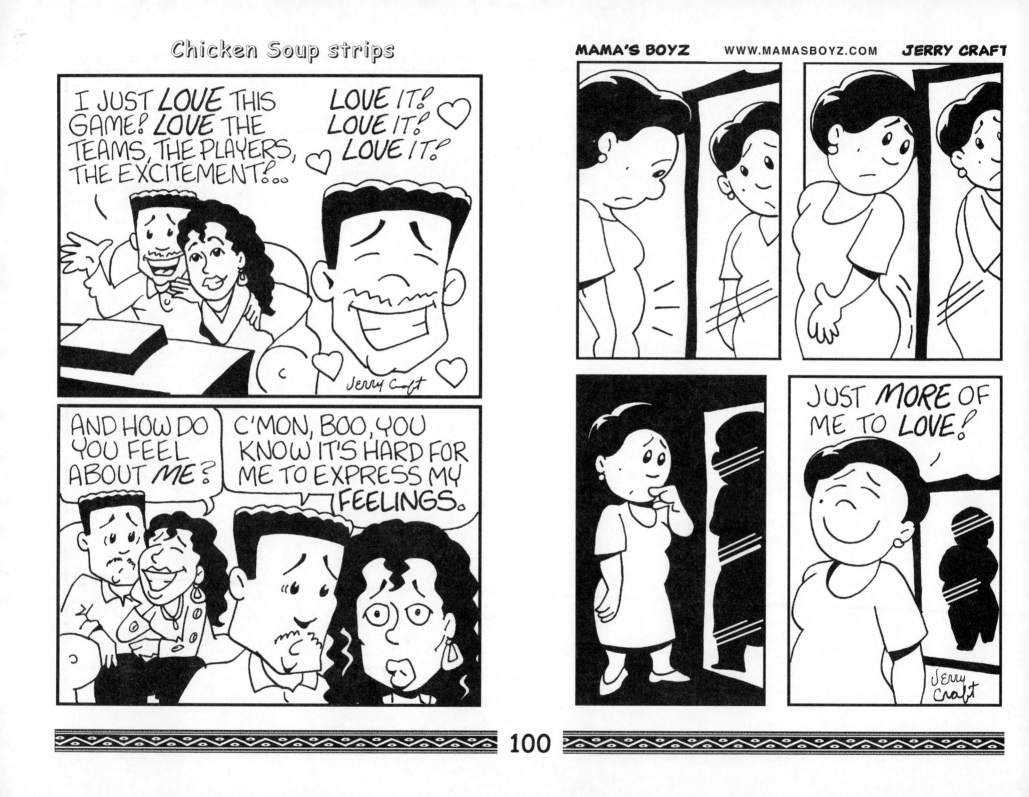

ADIOS AMIGOS!

My, look at the time! Can you believe a year is up already? The Porter family and I really want to thank you for spending time with us. We hope you enjoyed hanging out with the family, and hopefully maybe even learned a thing or two. Remember, even if you don't like school, the education you get now will help to determine what you do as an adult.

Bad things like drinking, smoking and drugs will all come back to haunt you when you get older. Many adults can't get certain jobs now, or even vote, because of trouble that they got in when they were younger. A lot of the kids who did that when I was growing up aren't doing too well now. And unfortunately, many of them never even got a chance to clean up their act.

It's hard enough to succeed without stacking the deck against yourself. So try hard, surround yourself with good people, get an education, and most of all, set goals for yourself. Real friends not only support you when you're not doing well, but they stand by you when you're successful, too. And they are actually happy for you without trying to drag you down. Anyone who does not want to see you do well, and does things to get you in trouble or block your success is NOT a friend. Remember, the decisions you make from this day on, can matter for the rest of your life.

Thanks for spending time with us, we hope you had as much fun as we did.

Best to you always,

Mom, Tyrell, Yusuf, Gran'pa, Uncle Greg and your pal, Jerry Craft

photo by Autier Craft

111

MAMA'S BOYZ ORDER FORM

(You don't actually have to cut this page out, I always hated cutting stuff out of my books)

To order additional copies of MAMA'S BOYZ- HOME SCHOOLIN'
please order online at www.mamasboyz.com or send a check or money order made out to
Jerry Craft for $9.95 ($14.95 in Canada) plus $3.50 ($4.50 in canada) shipping and handling
for the first book and $1.00 shipping for each additional book to:

**Jerry Craft
PMB #114 b, 304 Main Ave
Norwalk, CT 06851**

Connecticut residents please add 6% sales tax. (I'm not picking on you guys, it's the law!)

And unfortunately, since I know a lot of you slept through math class, I will break it down for you:
One book is $9.95 plus $3.50. Total $13.45
Two books are 2 x $9.95 ($19.90) plus $4.50 shipping. Total $24.40
Three books are 3 x $9.95 ($29.85) plus $5.50 Shipping. Total $35.35

Don't forget to **CLEARLY** write or type your name, address and phone number and send it along with your payment. Checks with no mailing addresses will be considered donations. And really appreciated! Also, if you want me to autograph it to someone, you have to tell me who to make it out to, or else I'll just use my own kids' names. You can also order this book, the first Mama's Boyz book, and Mama's Boyz t-shirts, sweatshirts,mugs and other stuff online at www.mamasboyz.com
Thank you for your support!

ATTENTION ORGANIZATIONS:
Mama's Boyz books are available at quantity discounts with bulk purchase for educational, business or sales promotion use. For information e-mail me at jerrycraft@aol.com